Bears, Scares and Underwear

Charlie Bacon

Bears, Scares and Underwear

by Gary Hogg

ILLUSTRATED BY ELISE SUMMERS

Little Buckaroo Books

Text copyright © 2013 by Gary Hogg
Illustrations copyright © by Elise Summers
Designed by Matt Shay
ISBN 978-0-93077-136-2

Printed in the U.S.A.

10 9 8 7 6 5 4 3 2 1

For Emily,
the star at the top of my family tree.

Contents

Chapter 1

Something Fishy

"Something smells fishy around here," said Mrs. Bacon. She turned off the vacuum and started sniffing the living room.

"It's Jimmy," said Charlie, pointing to his little brother. "I think he had an 'accident' in his shorts."

"Nice try, Charlie," said Mrs. Bacon, "but the smell is from your direction. Are you wearing that shirt?"

"Shirt? What shirt?" asked Charlie, quickly zipping his jacket.

"You know very well what I'm talking about," insisted Charlie's mother. "Your stinks-like-a-dead-fish shirt."

"Oh, you mean my lucky shirt?" asked Charlie. "I haven't seen that old thing since you said to throw it out."

Mrs. Bacon crossed over to her son and unzipped his jacket. The smell almost knocked her over. She backed off quickly. "Charlie, why on earth do you wear that disgusting shirt?"

"I have to," pleaded Charlie. "Grandpa said in order to catch a fish you have to stink like one."

"He did not say that! You have to think like a fish," insisted Mom.

But Mom, this shirt really works," begged Charlie. "Last time I wore it was my best fishing day ever. Grandpa said the fish were following me. This shirt has special powers."

"It has special powers all right," joked Charlie's mom. "Anyone who gets within a mile of it gets a sick stomach."

"It doesn't bother Grandpa," said Charlie, zipping up his jacket.

"All right, if you want to wear the smelliest shirt in town, go wait for your grandpa outside," said Mrs. Bacon.

Charlie's mother resumed vacuuming. Charlie grabbed his backpack and fishing pole and went out.

Across the street Charlie spotted a big puddle in front of the Winwood's house. He flipped the end of his fishing pole back and cast at the water. His fishing line only waved in the air and dropped in front of his shoes.

"Not enough weight," observed Charlie. He opened his tackle box and dug out a large sinker. He fastened it to his line.

Charlie took his fishing rod in both hands. He slowly lifted it over his shoulder and zipped it forward as hard as he could. The hook sailed across the street and into the Winwood's open window.

"Oops," said Charlie. For once, he hoped he wouldn't catch anything. He jerked the fishing pole, reeling for all he was worth.

The screams that came from the Winwood's house might have scared a lesser fisherman. Not Charlie! He just reeled faster.

What he didn't know was that the hook had caught the back of Mrs. Winwood's dress and Charlie had been reeling her in. Hearing his wife's wild screams, Mr. Winwood had charged to her rescue and grabbed her just before she was pulled through the window.

The hook broke free and Mr. Winwood slammed the window shut and pulled down the shade.

"The big ones always get away," mumbled Charlie as he finished reeling in his line.

The sound of Grandpa honking the horn of the truck erased the incident from Charlie's mind. He ran in the house, shouting, "They're here!"

Mrs. Bacon gave Charlie a good-bye kiss. "Be careful," she said.

"Always," replied Charlie. "See you tomorrow night."

Grandma had the truck door open and was waving to her only daughter. Grandpa never came in to visit on a fishing day.

Charlie jumped in the truck and they headed for the hills. Grandpa didn't like to keep hungry fish waiting.

Chapter 2
Picture This

"I can tell you're wearing that lucky fishing shirt," said Grandma, rolling down her window and gasping for air.

"That's my boy," said Grandpa.

"Hey, Grandpa," said Charlie grinning, "do you think it will bring us enough luck to catch Old Moby Trout?"

Moby Trout was the biggest and smartest fish in Pineview River. Grandpa had already dedicated three years to catching it.

"I won't rest until that fish is mounted over my fireplace," Grandpa would tell anyone who would listen.

Grandpa had hooked him twice but both times the mighty fish had broken the line and escaped.

"It's going to take more than luck to catch old Moby. I'd say we're going to need some kind of miracle," said Grandpa.

"A miracle," repeated Charlie softly.

"Martha, push that mirror out a little," said Grandpa. "I can't see past the back of the trailer."

Grandpa called his camping trailer Paradise on Wheels. Grandma called it Parasite on Wheels. Every camping trip she vowed to stay home, but Grandpa always talked her into coming.

"It wouldn't be a vacation without you," he always said.

"Of course it wouldn't," she'd snap back. "If I didn't come, you'd have to do your own cooking and cleaning."

Grandpa and Grandma argued a lot, but they actually seemed to enjoy each other. Charlie loved joining their fishing trips. He always hoped he would see some real wildlife, like a grizzly bear or a mountain lion or even Bigfoot.

Charlie felt sure this was his lucky trip. He felt so lucky that he had borrowed his sister's camera to document his wildlife encounter. Borrow was not actually the right word, since Shrudi didn't know Charlie had her camera.

Charlie had a simple plan. He would keep the camera until Shrudi started to look for it. He'd let her storm about the house screaming until the whole family was sick to death of her. Then, like a hero, he would suddenly "find" the missing camera. His parents would be so relieved when Shrudi shut up they would probably raise his allowance.

"If we see Bigfoot, will you take a picture of me with the big fella?" Charlie asked.

"Sure," laughed Grandpa. "I brought a deck of cards; maybe we could get a picture of you two playing cards."

"Awesome!" cried Charlie. He tried imaging it. He could see the headlines: **Charlie Bacon Beats Bigfoot at Cards.**

"It was tough going," Charlie would tell the reporter. "I had to keep the big brute from looking at my cards. He smelled like garbage and was a cheat too."

Charlie snapped back to reality and asked Grandma if she wanted to be in the picture. She burst out laughing and said, "The only smelly creature I want to pose with is your grandfather."

Grandpa pulled out two very old, very hard sticks of black licorice from under the seat. He popped one

in his mouth and handed Charlie the other. Charlie put the stick in his mouth and began sucking. Black licorice made him feel tough. He especially liked how the juice turned his teeth black.

Charlie rose up to look in the mirror. His teeth were as black as midnight. He gave Grandpa a big, toothy smile. Grandpa grinned back. The licorice had turned his teeth black too.

"Let's sing some camping songs," suggested Grandma as Grandpa turned off the main road and headed for Pineview Campground.

"I know a great one," said Charlie excitedly. "It's called Greasy Grimy Gopher Guts."

Before Charlie could begin, Grandpa was singing it. He knew every word.

"I've known that little ditty since your mom was a girl," said Grandpa. "She used to love it."

Charlie couldn't believe his ears. "My mom?" he asked. "She nearly faints if I even say barf."

"Well, at one time your mother was the queen of gross songs," chuckled Grandpa.

"Wow," said Charlie.

The travelers were singing merrily when Grandpa suddenly hit the brakes. Standing smack in the middle of the road was a giant moose.

Chapter 3

Milton and the Moose

Grandpa honked the horn while Charlie scrambled to grab Shrudi's camera.

"Stop that, Milton," urged Grandma. "You're scaring it."

Grandpa honked again and the moose started up the hill along the road. "The poor thing can't make it up that steep hill," cried Grandma.

Grandpa scoffed, "Moose are very surefooted." Suddenly, the giant beast started sliding down the hill.

"Look Grandpa, he's skiing," joked Charlie.

Grandpa didn't laugh. He was trying to shift gears. The moose came sliding straight for the truck.

17

"Floor this jalopy!" screamed Grandma. "It's going to hit us!"

Grandpa still couldn't find first gear. CRASH! The moose landed on the hood, his big lips smashed up against the windshield. The dazed animal just lay there like a gigantic hood ornament.

"Awesome!" shouted Charlie.

Grandpa threw open the door and climbed out. "OK, twinkle toes, let's move it," ordered Grandpa. The moose didn't move, so Grandpa gave him a poke. The moose wouldn't budge.

"Maybe he sprained an ankle," offered Grandma. "Get up there and help him, Milton."

Reluctantly, Grandpa climbed on the hood next to the moose. "OK, big guy, enough funny business. Get off my truck," said Grandpa. He grabbed the moose's antlers and shook them. The moose just grunted.

Grandpa decided to try the rear end. Straddling the animal, he picked up the tail and began pulling. Charlie, trying to be helpful, laid on the truck's horn. The blast shot a bolt of fear through the beast. It leaped to its feet with Grandpa on its back.

Before Grandpa could get off, the huge animal jumped off the truck. Grandpa was flat on the moose's back. His hands were gripping the tail and his feet were locked under the antlers. He was screaming like a little girl on a wild carnival ride as the giant beast went round and round. With a loud grunt, the moose stopped spinning and started bucking like a rodeo bull.

"Grandma yelled, "Get off! Get off!"

"I'm trying! I'm trying!" screamed Grandpa as he bounced up and down on the mad moose. Suddenly, the moose stopped bucking and froze in place. Its eyes were wild and it was panting hard.

Grandpa quickly sat straight up. But before he could get off, the moose lowered its head and took off up the road. Grandpa started screaming again as he bounced on the galloping beast.

"He's going to get himself killed," Grandma blurted as she took off after the runaway moose.

The moose left the road and ducked under a tree before running off. Grandpa was left dangling from a branch.

"Are you all right?" yelled Grandma.

"Do I look like I'm all right? I'm stuck in a tree, for crying out loud," shouted Grandpa.

"Can you climb down, or should I call for help?" asked Grandma.

"Of course, I can get down," grouched Grandpa. As he put his weight onto a short branch, there was a loud crack and the branch snapped. Grandpa fell out of the tree and landed on his back in the dirt.

Charlie raced over to Grandpa to get a close-up picture. Grandpa's face was red and his eyes were crossed.

"I showed that moose who was boss," said Grandpa as he sat up. "He'll think twice before messing with me again."

"I'll bet his ears are still hurting from all your screaming," joked Grandma as she helped her husband to his feet.

Grandpa limped to the road. "Did you get a picture of me riding that brute?" he asked.

"I filmed the whole thing," said Charlie.

"Good," said Grandpa, continuing up the road. "I want to see the fear in that moose's eyes."

Grandma slid into the driver's seat and announced,

"You're in no shape to drive. I'm taking the wheel."
Grandpa didn't argue and Grandma drove them to
Pineview Campground.

Chapter 4
The Wrath of Granny

Grandma backed the trailer into the first empty camping spot and turned off the engine.

Grandpa got out and took a deep breath. "It's great to be back. Let's go check out the river while Grandma sets up," he said, looking around for Charlie.

Charlie was already gone. He was skipping rocks across the water when Grandpa arrived. "What are you doing?" hollered Grandpa. "You'll scare the fish."

"The water is so smooth, I just had to skip a few," answered Charlie.

"I see what you mean," said Grandpa. He picked up a nice flat stone and let it fly. That rocked skipped halfway across the river, hit a boulder sticking out from the water and kept flying. It shot clear to the other side and then bounced off a fisherman's head.

"Hey, what are you doing?" screamed the man.

"Calm down, it was an accident," answered Grandpa. "You should have ducked."

"I'll report you to the park ranger," shouted the man.

"The park ranger? Why don't you go tell Mommy?" teased Grandpa.

Charlie tugged at his grandpa's shirt. "Let's get out of here."

"Relax, Charlie," said Grandpa. "What's he going to do—swim across the river?"

"He doesn't need to," said Charlie. "He has a boat."

"What?" said Grandpa.

"He has a boat and he's climbing into it," replied Charlie. "Should I throw some rocks at him?"

"No more rocks," snapped Grandpa. "If he wants a fight, I guess that's just what he'll get."

Grandpa rolled up his sleeves and started cracking his knuckles. The boat moved quickly across the glassy river. Just then Grandma came marching up the trail.

"There you are," she said. "Who's ready for some bird watching?"

"Martha, go back to the trailer," Grandpa ordered.

The splashing oars caught Grandma's attention. "Why is that man rowing like his pants are on fire?" she asked.

"He wants to kill Grandpa," Charlie answered.

"Anyone out to kill your grandfather will have to line up behind me," said Grandma.

The boat hit the shore and the man jumped out. He put up his fists and started toward Grandpa. "Come on, you old goat," he goaded.

Grandma stepped between the two men. She poked the angry man in the chest and announced, "Milton has had enough excitement for one day."

"Look who's hiding behind Mommy," teased the man.

Grandma's eyes grew big, "Do I look like this old geezer's mother?"

"Lady, these rocks are younger than you," said the man.

"Why, you little twerp," snarled Grandma. She grabbed an oar from the boat and began swatting the man's rear end. He jumped in the river and swam away faster than a fish. Grandma chucked the oar after him and shoved his boat into the water.

"I had everything under control," growled Grandpa. "I was about to teach that whippersnapper a lesson he'd never forget."

"You can teach him how easy it is to make old people bleed some other time," teased Grandma.

Grandpa snorted and headed for camp. Charlie began to follow when Grandma stopped him. "Hold it right there, young man, we have birds to watch," she called.

"Birds are boring," Charlie said. "I want to go fishing."

"There's plenty of time for fishing," Grandma insisted. "I want to look for a yellow-bellied sapsucker before it gets too hot."

Grandpa marched toward the campsite. Charlie turned and followed Grandma. They hiked to the top of a hill and began looking for birds.

"Shhh," hushed Grandma. "Listen for a bird's song."

There was a soft whistle coming from the pine tree to their left. Charlie spotted it first. It was a bright yellow bird about halfway up the tree.

"A yellow warbler," whispered Grandma.

A dark red bird landed in the tree in front of them. Grandma thumbed through her book. "A red crossbill," she said softly.

Charlie was starting to get the hang of bird watching. They hiked farther down the trail and spotted a scarlet tanager and a mountain bluebird. He was looking through the binoculars when he saw three huge black birds slowly circling.

"Are those eagles?" he asked.

Grandma took the binoculars and focused on the birds. "Vultures," she said. "They're flying over our camp. They must be looking for lunch."

"What do they eat?" asked Charlie.

"Dead things." answered Grandma.

"We better go check on Grandpa," suggested Charlie.

"You're right," said Grandma. "There's no telling what kind of trouble he's cooking up."

Chapter 5

Bear Scare

As they hiked into camp, Charlie spotted smoke billowing out the trailer's door.

"Looks like your grandfather's cooking," said Grandma.

Charlie raced to the trailer. He could smell bologna frying. In no time his mouth was watering for one of Grandpa's famous fried bologna and onion sandwiches. Grandma grimaced as she stepped into the trailer and saw the huge mess.

Grandpa handed her a sandwich and said, "A little piece of heaven for my angel."

They all sat down and had just bitten into their

greasy sandwiches when a big voice boomed from right outside of their trailer. "Is everything all right in there?"

"Just having a little lunch," called back Grandpa.

A park ranger popped his head in through the open door. "I saw the smoke and got a little worried," said the ranger.

"Just a little burnt bologna," said Grandpa. "We've got an extra sandwich if you're hungry."

"No thanks," said the ranger. "Be sure and store all of your food inside your truck or trailer. We've had a

bear sighting earlier this week."

Grandma sat straight up. "I'm terrified of bears!" she exclaimed.

"They usually keep their distance," said the ranger. "If you come in contact with one, try to remain calm and do not run. Make loud noises by yelling or hitting two rocks together. If the bear isn't scared off, walk slowly backward while avoiding eye contact with the bear."

"You've got it," said Grandpa.

The ranger headed to the next campsite while Charlie and his grandparents ate their lunch. After wolfing down two sandwiches, Grandpa patted his tummy and yawned, "How about we have a little siesta?"

"A nap?" groaned Charlie. "I'm not sleepy. I'll be outside if you need me."

Grandma looked worried. "You heard the ranger.

There may be bears in the area. Stay close to the trailer," she warned.

"I promise," said Charlie, closing the trailer door. He plopped down on a grassy spot under the shade of a tall pine tree. "Old people sleep too much," he said, yawning. "When I'm old, I'll never sleep. Never, never, never." By the third 'never,' Charlie's eyes were lead heavy. Soon he was snoring.

"Wake up, sleepy head," said Grandpa, kicking Charlie's foot. "Do you think I brought you all the way up here to sleep?"

"Are we going after Moby Trout now?" asked Charlie, snapping awake.

"You bet," said Grandpa. "But first I have a little sneaky work for us to do. Grandma is still snoozing. I think she needs a couple of bears to get her blood pumping. Are you up to it?"

Charlie answered with his best bear growl.

"Good," said Grandpa. "Let's go."

The two bears growled and pawed the trailer. Soon they had it rocking back and forth. A mighty loud commotion rattled inside the trailer and then all was quiet. Grandpa sneaked around the side and threw open the door. A bloodcurdling scream nearly knocked him over. There, standing on the bed, holding a frying pan, was Grandma.

"Hello sweetheart," said Grandpa. "Expecting company?"

Grandma took one look at Grandpa's smiling face and screamed again. Grandpa ducked as the frying pan flew past his head. Next, out came the kettle, three plates, and the washbasin.

"Head for the hills," cried Grandpa. "She's gone berserk!"

Charlie dove behind a large rock and Grandpa hid behind a log.

"You all right?" asked Grandpa.

"I think so," answered Charlie. "For a minute, I thought wc were goners."

"She'll calm down soon enough," said Grandpa.

"I hope so," complained Charlie. "She has all the food."

"Is that your worry?" asked Grandpa. "Charlie, the woods are Mother Nature's restaurant. We're surrounded by delicacies to eat."

"Like what?" asked Charlie.

"Like, uh, let's see," said Grandpa, looking around. "Like gum. You like gum, don't you?"

"Yeah," replied Charlie. "Do you have some?"

"Sure," said Grandpa with a wink. He walked over to the tall pine tree and chipped off two pieces of dried sap with his pocketknife. He handed Charlie a piece and popped the other in his mouth.

"Now just chew on the wonder of nature," said Grandpa.

The two outdoorsmen stood there chomping slowly.

"It doesn't taste like gum," mumbled Charlie.

"Give it a chance," said Grandpa.

Charlie and his grandfather screwed up their faces as the bitter juice filled their mouths. Finally, Grandpa spit out his gum. "Forget it," he said, gagging. "That tastes horrible. I'm getting dizzy."

"Me too," choked Charlie. He spit his gum and rubbed his tongue along his shirt sleeve.

Grandpa headed for the trailer with Charlie right behind him.

"Martha," shouted Grandpa. "We need something

to drink. It's an emergency."

The door opened slowly.

"Glad to see you've come to your senses," said Grandpa. As he stepped up, a pan of water hit him in the face. Grandpa bent to wipe his eyes and a second wave hit Charlie.

"There, that ought to keep you for awhile," said Grandma, slamming the trailer door.

"I don't think she's cooled down," said Charlie.

Suddenly, the door opened again and two sleeping bags came flying out.

"What?" cried Grandpa.

"Wouldn't want you to catch cold out there with your friends the bears," said Grandma. The door shut and the lock clicked.

"Looks like we're sleeping under the stars tonight," said Grandpa. "Really, she's doing us a favor. We'll take what these wild woods dish out and lap it up like the mountain men we are."

"Right," said Charlie, "we'll lap it up. So long as it doesn't taste like that tree sap. That stuff is the worst."

"You got that right," said Grandpa, sticking out his tongue.

The two mountain men took their sleeping bags and went looking for a camping spot.

Chapter 6

Ants in Your Pants Boogie

"This looks like a good place," declared Grandpa. "We'll spread out that pile of pine needles to make a soft bed."

Grandpa and Charlie got on all fours and started smoothing out the gigantic pile. In no time, they were covered with crawling, biting ants.

"It's an ant hill!" screamed Charlie.

Grandpa jumped to his feet and started dancing like a wild man. Charlie scrambled to his feet and joined Grandpa in the ants in your pants boogie. They were jumping, spinning, and slapping like two maniacs.

After the ant dance, Grandpa sat down on a log to catch his breath. Charlie plopped down next to him.

"Those ants were almost as mad as Grandma," grumbled Charlie. "I think we should go apologize to her."

"We're not going to let some little ants keep us from a night in the woods," said Grandpa.

He stood up, grabbed his sleeping bag, and hiked farther up the trail. He found an open area between some bushes and tall trees. After inspecting it for ant hills, he announced, "We'll leave our sleeping bags here while we hunt up some grub."

"How do we do that?" asked Charlie.

"Just watch the old master," answered Grandpa. "We'll be eating like kings tonight. How does a big fish dinner sound?"

"Great, but how can we fish?" asked Charlie.

"Grandma has our poles."

"There's more than one way to catch a trout," replied Grandpa confidently.

Grandpa led Charlie down the trail to the river.

"First, we make sure no predators are stalking the water," said Grandpa.

"You mean like that guy who tried to beat you up?" asked Charlie.

"No," replied Grandpa. "I mean bears."

"Oh boy! I hope we see one," said Charlie excitedly. "I want to get my picture with one."

"Bears are dangerous, wild animals," said Grandpa seriously. "You heard the ranger. If we see one, we are to remain calm, make loud noises, and get out of its way."

Grandpa looked up and down the river. After making sure there were no wild animals, he cut two straight branches off a nearby tree.

"These should work," said Grandpa, snapping off the leaves. He sharpened the small ends while Charlie watched.

"Here you go, Charlie, your very own fishing spear," said Grandpa.

"Excellent!" shouted Charlie. "We're having fish kabobs."

The two mountain men took off their shoes and socks, grabbed their spears, and waded into the cold water. "Be careful," Grandpa warned, "these rocks are slippery. I don't want to have to fish you out of here."

"I won't fall," said Charlie, peering into the water. "Everything looks fuzzy. How can we spot any trout?"

"Just move slowly and think like a fish," said Grandpa.

All at once, Grandpa raised his stick high in the air.

Charlie held his breath. Grandpa thrust his spear into the water, but it came down on a rock and broke in half.

"Don't let that fish get away," shouted Grandpa.

Charlie started stabbing the water. "I got him!" he screamed.

"You got me!" bellowed Grandpa, grabbing his harpooned foot. Grandpa tried to hop to shore, but on his second hop, he slipped on a rock and splashed backward into the river.

Rushing to the rescue, Charlie tripped on his spear and tumbled in headfirst. The two sportsmen thrashed about the water until at last they reached the shore.

"Are you all right?" gasped Grandpa.

"Yeah," said Charlie. "What about your foot?"

"Hurts like the dickens," moaned Grandpa. "But it's not bleeding."

"Now what?" asked Charlie.

"We dry off the best we can," said Grandpa, wiping his face with a sock. "Then we get some real chow."

"You mean we beg Grandma to take us back?" asked Charlie, hoping.

"Absolutely not," snorted Grandpa. "We look in the truck for crumbs."

Under the truck's seat they found one stick of black licorice, a peanut butter cookie, and a peppermint candy covered with fuzz.

"We'll split the cookie and flip a coin for the licorice," said Grandpa.

Charlie lost the coin toss. He looked down at his measly dinner. He decided to eat the cookie and save the candy for a midnight snack.

"We might as well turn in," said Grandpa. "We're way too soggy to do anything else."

The fearless campers laid their damp clothes to dry on some rocks. Wearing only underwear, they slid into their warm sleeping bags.

Charlie spotted the first star of the night. "Star bright, star light, first star I see tonight," he said softly.

"What did you wish for?" asked Grandpa.

"I wished you'd tell me a scary story," said Charlie.

"Your wish is granted," said Grandpa. "Buckle up for a ghost story."

Chapter 7

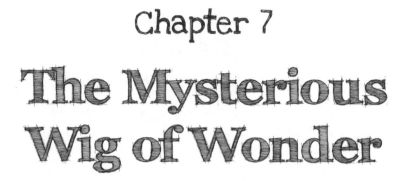

"This is the story of the Fisherman's Ghost," said Grandpa in a spooky voice. Charlie snuggled deeper into his sleeping bag.

"Once upon a river, there was a fisherman named Ernie McFadden. He was the best fisherman in all the land. His secret was he only fished at night and he used magical worms for bait."

"Magical worms? Were they ninja worms?" Charlie asked.

"Not exactly," said Grandpa.

"Did they have superpowers and fancy names like Wormonator and Slime Master? Did they zap the fish with laser beams?" Charlie asked louder.

"They were delicious so fish loved them," said
Grandpa.

"Being delicious isn't much of a magical power.
What's the use of having magical powers if in the end
you just get eaten?" asked Charlie.

"Can I get back to my story?" asked Grandpa in a grumpy voice.

"OK, but it would be better with ninja fighting worms," suggested Charlie.

Grandpa cleared his throat and started again. "Once upon a river, there was a fisherman named Ernie McFadden. He was the best fisherman in the land. His secret was he only fished at night and used magical, ninja fighting, superhero, laser-shooting worms for bait."

Charlie gave a quiet cheer and Grandpa continued. "Each night Ernie would come home with a basket full of trout. He would always stop and give the biggest fish to the old lady that lived at the end of the lane. The next morning there would be another cup of magical worms on his doorstep.

"This continued for many weeks. One foggy night

in October, Ernie was greedy and kept all the fish for himself. The next morning there was only one worm on his doorstep. It was a huge bloodred night crawler."

"Was it an evil, blood-sucking, vampire worm?" Charlie asked.

"Why yes," said Grandpa. "It was an evil, blood-sucking, vampire worm."

"I knew it," said Charlie.

"That night when Ernie went fishing, he wrapped the large night crawler around his hook," said Grandpa.

"Did it sneak off the hook and bite Ernie McFadden on the neck and suck out all his blood and is that how he became a ghost?" Charlie asked.

Grandpa thought for a minute and then said, "Yes, that is exactly how it happened. The End."

"Awesome story," whispered Charlie. "Tell me

another one."

Grandpa yawned and said, "Just one more, but no interrupting."

"I promise," said Charlie.

"When I was a boy about your age, I was best friends with Harvey Wills. He was a freckled-faced troublemaker. On a hot Saturday afternoon we were as bored as a couple of carrots in a candy store. We decided to open our own museum in my backyard. We called it the Morbid Museum of the Macabre.

"Macabre was Harvey's idea. He said it was a smart way to say we had lots of gross and dead stuff," explained Grandpa.

"We had a skeleton exhibit that contained some mouse and fish bones. There was the Evil Eye exhibit. It was a large marble painted to look like an eyeball. Our Cursed Dirt of Death display was a cup of dirt that we got from the cemetery.

"The highlight was the Bugs of Doom exhibit. Our star was a huge stink bug that we named Bugzilla. We billed him as the world's smelliest stink bug. Harvey said one spray of Bugzilla's powerful stink would cause immediate projectile vomiting.

"Business was horrible. The only customer was Harvey's cousin Neal and he demanded his money back when he saw the cup of dirt. He said his sister's face was ten times scarier than anything we had in our dumb museum.

"We decided to take our show on the road. We loaded everything up and took it to school on Monday. We figured some of the little kids would be willing to use their lunch money to see the Morbid Museum of the Macabre.

"We set up our stuff at recess. Lots of kids gathered

around but no one would pay. That's when Harvey came up with the world's worst idea. He announced that I was going to be performing a vomit-defying stunt. I would keep Bugzilla on my tongue for one full minute. That turned things around quickly. Money started pouring in.

"I opened my mouth wide, and Harvey placed the huge black bug on my tongue. The seconds ticked by and Bugzilla sat quietly on my extended tongue. When kids started chanting, 'Stink! Stink! Stink!' the principal, Mr. Walker, marched over to see what was going on. I quickly closed my mouth. Bugzilla didn't like it when the lights went out. I could feel him crawling farther down my throat.

"I spit the huge bug out like a giant loogie. Bugzilla landed in Principal Walker's hair. Harvey grabbed the bug and yanked. He not only had hold of Bugzilla, he had some of the principal's hair in his hand too. None of us knew that Mr. Walker wore a wig. We were all shocked to see Harvey holding the principal's hair. Harvey panicked and threw the hair in the air.

"It landed in the middle of the road. Before anyone could get to it, a dog snatched the wig and ran off. Mr. Walker's face turned lava red. He was furious. We had to spend every recess for a week scrubbing toilets."

Charlie laughed until his side ached. "Whatever happened to the principal's hair?" he asked between giggles.

"Harvey recognized the dog that took the wig. We hunted him down and found out where he buried the hair. We dug it up and put it in our Morbid Museum of the Macabre. We called it The Mysterious Wig of Wonder, but everyone knew it was the principal's hair. Kids paid a nickel to touch it and ten cents to try it on. It was a real money maker," said Grandpa.

"Someday I'm going to have my own Morbid Museum," said Charlie.

"I'll be one of your first customers," said Grandpa. "We better get some shut eye. Tomorrow we're going to catch Moby Trout."

Chapter 8

Things That Go Bump in the Night

"Grandpa, wake up," whispered Charlie. "There's something in the bushes." Charlie scooted his sleeping bag closer to Grandpa.

"Relax," said Grandpa. "Probably just a raccoon."

They heard a grunt followed by a mean growl.

"There it is again," said Charlie. "What if it's a bear?"

"Then we do what the ranger said. We remain calm and don't run," whispered Grandpa.

At that moment, the creature rushed out of the bushes, heading straight for Charlie and Grandpa. Grandpa burst from his sleeping bag as if he'd be shot from cannon. "Head for the trees," he shrieked. "It's a grizzly."

Charlie blasted out of his bag and charged after Grandpa. Charlie and his grandpa scrambled up a tree like a couple of frightened squirrels.

"I think we kept our cool pretty good," said Charlie, clinging to a branch. In the moonlight he could see Grandpa sitting in his polka dotted underwear on the branch next to him.

"You're right," said Grandpa. "I think we handled that like a couple of pros."

After several minutes, Charlie asked, "Do you think it's safe to climb down now?"

"I'm not budging until I know that man eater is gone," answered Grandpa.

"But we're in our underwear," said Charlie.

"I'd rather be in a tree in my underwear than in a grizzly's stomach," replied Grandpa.

Grandpa and Charlie tried to get comfortable and

then they drifted to sleep. The next morning, they were jarred awake by loud talking. "Look, Roger, there's something up in the top of that tree," said a lady.

"I don't see anything," replied the man.

"I see it," shouted a boy. "It's an old man and a kid in their underwear!"

"Roger, get the camcorder," directed the woman. "We've got to film this and post it on the Internet."

That was all Grandpa needed to hear. Charlie and Grandpa came slipping and sliding down the tree as fast as firemen. As they neared the bottom, Grandpa grabbed a large branch and swung into the air. Letting go, he fell into a pile of pine needles. He jumped to his feet and made a dash for the trailer.

"Hurry, Roger," shouted the lady. "The old one is getting away."

Charlie caught up to Grandpa at the trailer door. Grandpa threw open the door and the two runners dove into the trailer. Grandma was cooking bacon and eggs.

"Where are your clothes?" she asked.

Grandpa was out of breath. "W-W-W-e were attacked by a g-g-g-grizzly b-b-b-bear last night," he stuttered.

"And it made you run around the campground in your underwear?" asked Grandma.

Grandpa began to tell the story, but as he got to the part where the bear was ten feet tall, Charlie noticed that Grandma was biting her lip to keep from laughing.

"Grandpa, maybe the bear wasn't quite that big," suggested Charlie.

"What are you talking about?" snapped Grandpa. "That bear was a giant."

"Well, I'm thinking it was closer to Grandma's size," hinted Charlie.

Grandma burst out laughing. "You boys got what you deserved," she chuckled.

Grandpa's face turned red. "Martha, that is the lowest, dirtiest, most ornery trick you have ever pulled. I have half a mind to march out of here," he said, standing. "Are you coming, Charlie?"

Charlie picked up a piece of bacon and said, "I'm staying where I can eat this wonderful breakfast."

"On second thought, me too," said Grandpa, flashing Grandma a smile.

There was a knock at the door. While Charlie and Grandpa hurried to put on their clothes, Grandma opened the door.

"Sorry to bother you folks," said the ranger. "There's been another report of a bear. It caused quite a commotion last night."

Grandpa chuckled and said, "I can explain that. It wasn't a bear. It was my wife, Martha."

The ranger looked confused. "It was your wife?" he asked.

"There's nothing to worry about," said Grandma. "I was having a little fun and got carried away."

"You tore open trash bags with your teeth, rolled in the garbage, and then ate the spoiled food just for fun?" asked the ranger.

Grandma gasped, "Heavens no! I just pretended to be a bear to scare my husband."

"This wasn't a pretend bear. It made a huge mess," said the ranger. He handed Grandpa a card. "This has my name and cell phone number. Call me if you see any sign of a bear."

"We sure will," said Grandpa.

"And one more thing," added the ranger. "This is a family campground. You can't be running around in your underwear. Your neighbors showed me the footage they have of you on their video camera."

"Won't happen again," said Grandpa, quickly shutting the trailer door. The three campers sat down to the best breakfast Charlie ever had.

Chapter 9
A Fishing We Will Go

"Put on your lucky shirt and let's go fishing," barked Grandpa as Charlie swallowed the last piece of bacon. In no time, Charlie was dressed and waiting. He practiced sword fighting with his fishing pole while waiting for Grandpa outside the trailer.

Grandpa came out wearing his fishing vest, with hooks, lures, and fishing flies hanging like medals on a soldier's uniform. He looked like a five-star fishing general. "How's your shirt smell this morning?" he asked.

"Stinky as ever," replied Charlie, proudly.

"Great," said Grandpa. "Let's go catch some fish."

"Where do you think Moby is today?" asked
Charlie as they scrambled down the path.

"I know exactly where he is," replied Grandpa. "He's
in the beaver pond—just waiting to do battle."

The beaver pond was Grandpa's favorite fishing spot.
It was on a little stream that forked off the main river.

"What are you fishing with today?" asked Charlie

as they arrived at the beaver pond.

Grandpa laughed wickedly and declared, "Today, it's fly fishing."

"Excellent," said Charlie, moving off a bit. He knew better than to stand too near Grandpa's flying hook.

Soon, Grandpa was snapping his fishing line back and forth like a crazed cowboy with a bullwhip. But the day dragged on without any action. No nibbles. No bites. Nothing. By the time Grandma arrived, Grandpa and Charlie were thoroughly discouraged.

"It takes a woman's touch," said Grandma, pitching out a fishing line. "I've got one!" she instantly exclaimed. The fishing pole arched as a powerful fish pulled on the line.

"Reel him in," hollered Charlie, running to Grandma's side.

"I'm trying!" said Grandma excitedly.

Suddenly, the mighty fish flew out of the water. His body twisted hard as he splashed back in the pond.

"It's Moby Trout!" shouted Grandpa. "Quick, give me the pole."

"No way!" said Grandma. "This is my fish!"

The battle was awesome. Grandma would almost get him to the shore and then the giant fish would dive down deep. He jerked so hard he almost pulled Grandma into the water.

After what seemed like an hour, Grandma got Moby close enough for Charlie to net. The fish was so heavy Grandpa had to help Charlie pull it onto the shore. They took the hook from the trout's mouth and Grandpa hoisted him up.

"He's going to look great mounted over our fireplace," announced Grandpa.

"He most certainly will not," said Grandma,

grabbing the trout by the tail. "He's going right back in the water where he belongs."

"Are you crazy?" cried Grandpa, pulling Moby Trout back.

"I caught this fish. I'll decide what we do with him," argued Grandma.

While Grandpa and Grandma played tug of war with the fish, Charlie pulled out Shrudi's camera from his pack.

"Smile everybody," he said, snapping the picture. "Grandpa, you can hang this picture above your fireplace and we can put Moby back in the water."

"That's the perfect solution," said Grandma.

Grandpa bent over and put the gigantic fish in the pond. Moby Trout flapped his tail, splashing Grandpa in the face and swam off.

Charlie dashed back to camp. By the time his grandparents arrived, he had piled the fire pit with wood. "Can we roast hot dogs?" he asked.

"Sounds like a wiener to me," joked Grandma.

Grandpa started the fire while Charlie watched. "All my lucky shirt attracted today was flies," complained Charlie.

"Put on a clean shirt and you can cook the hot dogs," said Grandma.

Charlie tossed his fishing shirt on a log and raced in the trailer. He came out wearing a clean shirt and carrying a package of hot dogs. He crammed three hot dogs on a stick and thrust them in the fire. The flames quickly turned the wieners black.

"I hope you like your dogs well done," said Charlie, but as he spun around, the wieners flew off the stick and hit the ground. Charlie quickly picked them up before anybody noticed. He thought it best not to tell Grandpa and Grandma.

The three campers sat down to their lunch. Grandma took one nibble and exclaimed, "Look over there! Is that Bigfoot?"

While Charlie and Grandpa turned, Grandma threw her hot dog in some bushes.

"I don't see anything," said Grandpa.

"Me neither," added Charlie.

When Grandpa and Charlie turned back around, Grandma was wiping the corners of her mouth.

"Wow!" said Charlie. "You devoured your hot dog."

Grandma heard a bird's call and quickly got up to investigate. "That sounds like a hermit warbler," she said.

While she strolled to the other side of the camp, Charlie asked, "Do you want me to cook you another dog?"

"I couldn't eat another bite," answered Grandma.

"Well, I sure can," announced Charlie. "I'm going to eat five hot dogs. I'm as hungry as a…BEAR!"

Charlie jumped up shouting, "BEAR! BEAR! BEAR!"

Chapter 10

It Wants to Eat Me!

A black bear lumbered into the clearing. It was sniffing the air and heading straight for Grandma. The huge bear stopped at the bushes where Grandma tossed her hot dog. It found the discarded wiener and swallowed it in one gulp. The bear grunted, shook its head, and continued toward Grandma.

"Don't run," said Grandpa. "It might chase you. We'll try and scare it off."

Grandpa started clapping his hands and yelling while Charlie grabbed two rocks and banged them together. The slow-moving black bear paid no attention and stayed on course.

Grandma's voice quivered as she asked, "What should I do? It wants to eat me."

Grandpa shouted louder and waved his arms. The bear changed direction for a moment and then turned back toward Grandma. In desperation, Charlie grabbed his lucky shirt and threw it at the bear. It landed to the side of the huge animal.

The bear turned and sniffed the shirt. It grunted and buried its face in the stinky fabric. "It likes my shirt," called Charlie.

Grandpa opened the door to the trailer and motioned to Grandma. She slowly backed to the trailer and jumped in followed by Grandpa. Charlie was the last one in.

Grandma was still shaking as she called the park ranger. "There's a bear in our camp!" she shrieked. She provided the ranger with their campsite number and turned off the phone.

"He said we are to stay in our trailer and he'd be here as soon as possible," said Grandma.

The bear was in love with the smell of Charlie's fishing shirt. He pawed it, rubbed it, and rolled on it.

"He wants to wear my lucky shirt," said Charlie, laughing.

"Who would have guessed bears like fashion?" added Grandpa.

"That shirt smells like garbage," said Grandma. "He thinks there must be a rotten sandwich in the pocket."

Soon the park ranger arrived in a green truck and parked right in front of the trailer. He got out of his truck and opened the trailer's door. "Is anyone hurt?" he said, entering the trailer.

"We're fine, but I'm afraid my grandson's shirt is a total loss," reported Grandpa.

"I've called for assistance," said the ranger. "We're going to have to remove the bear from the area."

Three additional park rangers arrived. There was a steel cage on the back of their truck. After the rangers tranquilized the bear and put it safely in a cage, Grandpa, Grandma, and Charlie came out of the trailer.

"What are you going to do with him?" asked Charlie.

"Actually, he's a she," explained the ranger. "Female bears are called sows. We'll take her to the high country and release her."

The word traveled fast and soon other campers had gathered to get a look at the bear. Grandma announced to the crowd, "The bear was coming right for me but my grandson Charlie's fast thinking saved my life."

Charlie beamed and said, "Everything I know about camping I learned from my Grandpa. He's the best outdoorsman I know."

After the rangers drove off with the bear, the crowd slowly disappeared. Charlie picked up what was left of his lucky shirt.

"Do the world a favor and throw it in the fire," suggested Grandma.

"It's the first exhibit in my new Morbid Museum of the Macabre," said Charlie. "I'll call it the Shirt of Death. Now I just need to find a giant stink bug and I'll be ready to go home."

Grandma packed the trailer while Grandpa doused the fire. Under a log, Charlie found the biggest stink bug he had ever seen. "Meet Son of Bugzilla," he said, showing off his new prize.

"Did you have a good time?" asked Grandma

when they were all in the truck.

"This was my best camping trip ever," said Charlie beaming. "What about you, Grandpa?"

"Other than a sore back, a hundred ant bites, a harpooned foot, sleeping in a tree in my underwear, and a visit from a hungry bear I had a pretty good time too," replied Grandpa smiling.

They started singing Greasy Grimy Gopher Guts and headed for home.

About the Author

Gary Hogg is the author of more than twenty books. His hilarious stories include *Look What the Cat Dragged In, I Heard of a Nerd Bird*, and the popular *Spencer's Adventures* series. Gary says his fourth grade teacher inspired him to put his wild ideas into stories instead of acting them out in class. She kept her sanity and he became a writer. Of all the characters he's created, Gary says Charlie Bacon is the most like him.

Gary is a popular speaker and guest author. He has inspired over 2 million students to be better writers with his popular *Writing is Exciting!* assembly and workshop program. You can learn about him at **www.garyhoggbooks.com**.

Sneak Peek of Book 2

Charlie Bacon

Help! My Dad Is the Lunch Lady

It was the day before the school year began and Charlie Bacon had some complaints. He wanted to give himself a macho makeover for the new school year, but his parents had done everything in their power to stop him.

He wanted to shave his head. They said, "No way." He wanted to get a tattoo of a dragon. They said, "Absolutely not." He wanted to get a pen that wrote with blood and they threatened to have his head examined.

They wouldn't even let him get a new backpack. He'd had the same backpack since kindergarten. It was bright yellow and in the shape of a duck. You opened the beak to put things inside.

Charlie's best friend, Biff, came over to help him think of ways to pay for a new backpack.

"The tooth fairy is always a reliable source of money," suggested Biff.

"Why are teeth the only body part that gets a magical fairy?" asked Charlie. "Why isn't there an earwax fairy?"

"Or a hair fairy," added Biff. "Then my dad would be rich and bald instead of just bald."

"At least your dad has a job. All mine does is watch TV and cook," said Charlie.

"The tooth fairy always leaves me twenty dollars," bragged Biff.

Charlie got a brilliant idea. He'd put one of his teeth under Biff's pillow. The idea was the easy part. Finding a tooth to volunteer for fairy duty was going to be more difficult. Charlie got a long piece of heavy fishing line out of his dad's tackle box. He tied one end to his front tooth and fastened the other end to Biff's bike.

"You're going to have to ride super hard because permanent teeth are a lot harder to pull out than baby teeth," explained Charlie.

"Is there going to be blood?" asked Biff. "Seeing blood makes me vomit."

"Seeing vomit makes me vomit," Charlie said.

To keep the vomit at a minimum they decided it would be best if Biff kept his eyes closed during the extraction. Biff took off and crashed into a tree before the string was even tight.

"Maybe the tooth fairy will pay half price for a dog's tooth," suggested Biff.

Charlie's neighbor Mrs. Murphy had a bulldog

named Spud. He was sleeping in his doghouse, which made it easy for Charlie to tie the string to his tooth. They decided Biff should keep his eyes open this time. On the count of three, Biff took off. The only problem was that Spud had taken off at the count of two. He growled and took after Biff like he was going to kill him.

Charlie got on his bike and tried to catch them. After a couple of blocks the string fell off and Spud gave up. The boys stopped right in front of Dr. Carter's dentist office.

"Are you thinking what I'm thinking?" Charlie asked.

"Are you thinking about a dimension where you never have to change your underwear even after you've been chased by a crazy dog?" asked Biff as he tried to catch his breath.

"No," said Charlie, pointing at the dentist office. "Dr. Carter must throw away hundreds of teeth every day."

"You're a genius," said Biff.

They went to the back of the office. Biff boosted Charlie into the dumpster. That's when Charlie hit the jackpot. Sitting right on top was a gigantic golden tooth. He heaved it over the side of the dumpster and climbed out.

"There's no way that will fit under a pillow," said Biff.

Charlie opened the top of the ginormous plastic tooth. "It's the Treasure Tooth. Dr. Carter lets you pick a prize out of it, if you don't yell too much," he said.

"He must have gotten a new one because this hinge is busted," said Biff.

Charlie held the tooth up to Biff's back. "Perfect!"

he announced.

"What are you doing?" asked Biff.

"Checking out my new macho backpack," said Charlie.

"You can't wear a giant tooth to school," argued Biff.

"Watch me," replied Charlie.

"It doesn't even have straps," said Biff.

"That's why we're taking it to your house. Does your dad still have a closet full of duct tape?" asked Charlie.

"The Duct Tape King still rules," said Biff.